TOMMY ZOEWICKER,
the Pie Maker

ISBN 979-8-89345-086-6 (paperback)
ISBN 979-8-89345-087-3 (digital)

Christian Faith Publishing
832 Park Avenue
Meadville, PA 16335
www.christianfaithpublishing.com

Printed in the United States of America

TOMMY ZOEWICKER,
the Pie Maker

Janice Balo

Small Town, USA

1950s Summer

Once upon a time, there was a small little town, and in this small little town lived a young boy named Tommy Zoewicker, who was eleven years old. Every day, young Tommy would eat breakfast with his dad before he left for work. Tommy would walk out to the front sidewalk to tell his dad goodbye. Tommy would then go to meet his friends to play baseball at Ballers Park. Tommy wouldn't see his dad again until three o'clock when he came home from work. Every day, his mother would have a wonderful dinner ready for her family when his dad got home. He had a great mother and dad who loved him, and he felt loved.

School was out since it was summer, and he could do whatever he and his friends wanted to do. Most of the time, it was playing ball or going fishing. Every day was a fun day for Tommy.

But Friday was Tommy Zoewicker's favorite day. It was the day his mother baked. She would bake a different pie each week. Every week, Tommy would watch and help his mother when he could. Of all the pies and cakes his mother made, banana cream and lemon meringue were his favorite pies of all. He had watched his mother make pies for so long he thought that he could make both of those pies.

One day, Tommy had a great idea. He was going to ask his mother if he could make the banana cream and lemon meringue pies all by himself. He had the idea that he could take the pies to town on Saturday and sell them by the slice. Tommy was so happy when his mother said yes, he could make the pies. Tommy could hardly wait until next Friday when he and his mother would make their pies together. Tommy made two pies, one banana cream and one lemon meringue. They looked delicious.

On Saturday morning, Tommy got up, did his chores, and when he finished, he got his bicycle out of the garage and put the two pies in his basket and covered them with a towel.

Everyone in this small little town knew young Tommy Zoewicker. When Tommy rode into town, he set up beside a bench on the square. He had with him paper plates, plastic forks, and napkins because he was going to sell his pies by the slice. He was going to sell each slice for fifty cents.

*****

Tommy's pie business was doing great. Over time, everyone in town knew to expect young Tommy at the town square. Every week, he would sell both pies. He made six dollars every Saturday. When his pies were gone, he would ride home and put five dollars in his bank and keep one dollar for himself. Tommy knew that as well as his pies were selling, he would have to add another pie to his list.

Tommy had a lot of customers, but he had three who were very special to him that came every week to buy a slice of his homemade banana cream and lemon meringue pies. They would sit on the bench in the warm sunshine and eat their pie together. Tommy thought that they were such funny little old ladies. They always had a story to tell.

One Saturday, young Tommy arrived in town at twelve o'clock sharp. As usual, his customers were waiting for him, but he didn't see Cora, Emmily, or Harriet, who went by the nickname Hattie. They were all in their seventies, and all had white hair. On this Saturday, Cora, Emmily, and Hattie were late. When they had all gotten there, there was only one slice of lemon meringue left.

"Oh no, whatever are we going to do now?" said Hattie.

Cora, who was the oldest, said, "Since I'm the oldest, I should get the pie." This didn't go over very well with Emmily or Hattie.

Emmily said, "No, I'm the middle in age, and everyone knows that the middle child always gets left out."

When Emmily got done ranting and raving, Hattie said, "I'm the youngest. I always get my way. That piece of pie is mine."

All three ladies began to laugh and chuckle at themselves. They were acting childish. Young Tommy Zoewicker stood there and watched to see who was going to get the pie.

Finally Cora said, "I have an idea—we'll share the pie!"

Emmily said, "Why didn't I think of that?"

And Hattie said, "Because you wanted it all."

Tommy laughed with them and gave them one paper plate and three forks that he had left. Cora, Emmily, and Hattie took their forks and plates and were ready to dig into their pie.

All at once, Cora said, "Oh no, my fork is broken. Whatever am I going to do?" Then she looked down, and there on the ground lay a perfectly good used fork. She took her napkin, wiped it off, and said "This will do," but Emmily noticed it only had three prongs.

Cora shrugged her shoulders and said, "It will still work."

So all three ladies began eating their lemon meringue pie. In the end, everyone was happy, and so was Tommy Zoewicker with his six dollars.

*****

One day, a man traveling came to this small little town and thought, "What a quaint little town." The town was so clean, and everyone seemed to be so friendly as they waved at him as he drove by. The day was warm, and the sun was shining, so he decided to park his car and walk around the town for a while. It wasn't long until he came to the square of the small little town. As he looked around the square, he saw eight nice benches that any town would be proud to claim as their own. The man didn't know little Tommy Zoewicker, the pie maker, or anyone else for that matter. It was just a clean and friendly little town that he would like to come back and visit again someday.

*****

Now as stories go, after years of selling his special banana cream and lemon meringue pies, Tom Zoewicker had grown up to be a very special young man in the small town. Tom had saved his money and had decided to go to college. It was a sad day when Saturday came, and there were no more banana cream or lemon meringue pies to eat, and no more Tom Zoewicker. It was as if it was a day of mourning because everyone in town missed Tom and his pies.

One Saturday, the mayor and the town council got together and decided that they would do something special in honor of Tommy Zoewicker, as that was the way they thought of him. They decided that since Tom had made the town square so special for them, they would make the town square special for him. So the Small Town City Sidewalk Bench Manufacturer and the townspeople decided to pick a week during the summer and have a special Tommy Zoewicker Week celebration. The stores in the town would put their merchandise out on the sidewalks and have special sales, set up game booths, and have painted clowns parading around the square. Everyone was happy with the great ideas. Then, the Small Town City Sidewalk Bench Manufacturer came up with another idea to make the occasion even more special. They decided to put a plaque on the back of each of the eight benches around the small little town square to dedicate to young Tommy Zoewicker. The plaque on the back of each bench said, "In honor of Tommy Zoewicker, the Pie Maker."

The celebration in the small little town was a total success, and everyone was truly happy. Everyone in town had a great time and had much fun. The funniest thing they did was to dunk the mayor in the water dunking barrel. Everyone wanted to do that.

Each year, Tom would do his best to come to the celebration. He loved seeing all his old friends. Tom had done well in college. He had graduated from college with honors with a business degree. Now it was time to find the job of his dreams.

Tom liked the town that he had always lived in and decided that this was where he wanted to stay to give back to the small town that had given so much to him. In his search, it wasn't surprising that he found his perfect job. With his qualifications, Tom got his first real job at the Small Town City Sidewalk Bench Manufacturer. Eventually, he would become the vice president. He knew his hometown inside and out. Nothing could have gone better. A great life, a great job, and now to find the perfect wife. Tom was happy—yes, he was a happy man indeed.

For many years, Tom had in his mind that he would like to have a wife with blond hair and blue eyes. After all, wasn't that every man's dream? As Tom started watching the young ladies in town, he didn't notice that there was a pretty young lady who had her eyes on him.

One day, as Tom was sitting on one of the benches on the square, a pretty young lady came by and asked Tom if he minded if she sat down beside him for a while. They didn't talk much, since they were strangers to each other, but Tom couldn't help notice her red hair and green eyes. After a while, Tom introduced himself. He said, "Hi, my name is Tom," and she promptly told Tom her name. "My name is Rebecca, but everyone calls me Becky." After introductions were made, they sat there for a while and talked about how nice the weather was. It wasn't long before they each got up and went their separate ways.

Tom went back to work, but his mind kept wandering back to the girl he had met on his lunchtime break on the square. He thought of how pretty she was, but she didn't have blond hair. But oh, that red hair was beautiful. He hoped that he would see her again.

*****

Five days later, on Saturday, he decided to go to town and sit on the square again, on the same bench that had been dedicated to him. He hadn't been sitting there for long when—*Oh, what was her name again?* Then he remembered. *Rebecca! Yes, Rebecca, but she liked to be called Becky.* How lucky could he be? Becky came up to him and asked if she could sit down there for a while. She told Tom that she worked across the street at the local jewelry store. She was off for her lunchtime break, and of course, Tom didn't have to work on Saturdays. They struck up a conversation and got to tell each other a little bit about themselves.

Becky thought that Tom was a dream; he was so handsome. He would make some young lady a wonderful husband someday. She laughed to herself as she thought about it.

Tom didn't miss that smile. Those eyes sparkled like green diamonds when she smiled, and that red hair hung down in soft wavy curls to the middle of her back. He thought to himself how pretty she was and so sweet.

Tom decided to ask her if she would like to take a walk one day, and of course, she did, because she had her eyes on him for quite some time now. They decided on the next Saturday. They would meet here at this bench that had been built right here in his hometown by the Small Town City Sidewalk Bench Manufacturer. Tom didn't know that Becky knew quite a bit about him and that the eight benches on the square were dedicated to him. She kept that to herself.

*****

On the next Saturday, when Becky was off work, they strolled around the square. Tom wanted to ask Becky if she would like to go out some evening for dinner. This was a new experience for Tom, since they hadn't known each other for long; also, Tom had invested a great deal of his time in his work. Tom decided that he was going to have to be strong or possibly lose out altogether. He didn't want that, that was for sure. So with all the breath he had, he asked if she would like to go out to dinner one evening. Becky thought for a while, which made Tom nervous. She didn't want Tom to know that she had been waiting and wanting him to ask her out. She was beyond happy. They decided the next Friday night they would go out to the best little restaurant in town.

That night, they learned a lot about each other. They had both been born and raised here. They both loved their little town and wanted to live here for the rest of their lives. Becky was so pleasant and so easy to talk to. Tom thought that he'd better not let her slip away. He loved it when she laughed. Those green eyes would dance and sparkle. She made his heart skip a beat.

*****

Summer was quickly coming to an end, and fall was in the air. They had seen each other every Friday night and had become very close. Tom had started thinking about marriage. Becky was perfect for him. They liked the same things and the same places, but best of all, she wanted to live right here where he wanted to live. Tom decided he needed to buy an engagement ring, but he would have to go over to the next town since Becky worked in the only jewelry store in town. Tom thought that fall was a perfect time for a wedding. Not too hot, not too cold. Perfect. He had to buy the perfect ring for his perfect wife-to-be. He hoped.

On the next Saturday, Tom and Becky would meet at the bench where he had sold pies when he was young. He was going to have to tell Becky about that someday. It was a happy memory for him. Tom was nervous as he saw Becky crossing the street toward him. It was quitting time for Becky. They sat there for a while, just enjoying the warm fall day. Leaves were falling all around them. Becky noticed that Tom was more quiet than usual.

"Is anything wrong?" she asked.

"No," he said. In his mind, everything was perfect. "I'd like to ask you a question," Tom said.

In Honor of
TOMMY
ZOEWICKER

Tom stood up and pulled a box out of his jacket pocket. He kneeled down on one knee. He could hardly speak because of the lump in his throat and the beating in his heart. He took a long, slow breath and then said, "Becky, would you do me the honor of becoming my wife?"

Becky's hands went to her heart. She had been waiting for this moment, and now it was here. She was so happy she could not contain herself. She jumped up, threw her arms around his neck, and said, "Oh yes, yes, yes, I would love to be your wife. I love you so much."

And Tom told her how much he loved her. She loved the ring Tom had chosen for her; it was her style. It was happening, really happening, just the way he thought it would. Tom knew that it was not a blue-eyed blonde that he wanted, but this beautiful red-haired, green-eyed girl with a dimple in her right cheek when she smiled. Could life get any better than this? How could any man in the world be happier than him? Tom knew in his heart that this was love ever after. Just like a storybook tale where the bride and groom lived happily ever after, this was his "love ever after" story also.

They decided on a Christmas wedding. Then they would be husband and wife for the rest of their lives. Mrs. Tom Zoewicker—what a beautiful name! And she was his, all his.

Tom didn't think that there was ever a more beautiful woman than Becky Zoewicker. Who would ever imagine that a young Tommy Zoewicker, a pie maker, would end up marrying the most beautiful woman in town!

About the Author

Janice Balo lives in a 123-year-old house that her family calls home. They have lived there for fifty-five years, so they have a lot of memories. Janice is a wife of sixty-two years (where has the time gone?). She has four children, nine grandchildren, ten great-grandchildren, and two great-great-grandchildren. By the time this book is published, there will be one more great-grandson in their family. Her family is large and loved.